D0687199

THIS CANDLEWICK BOOK BELONGS TO:

_____

_____

_____

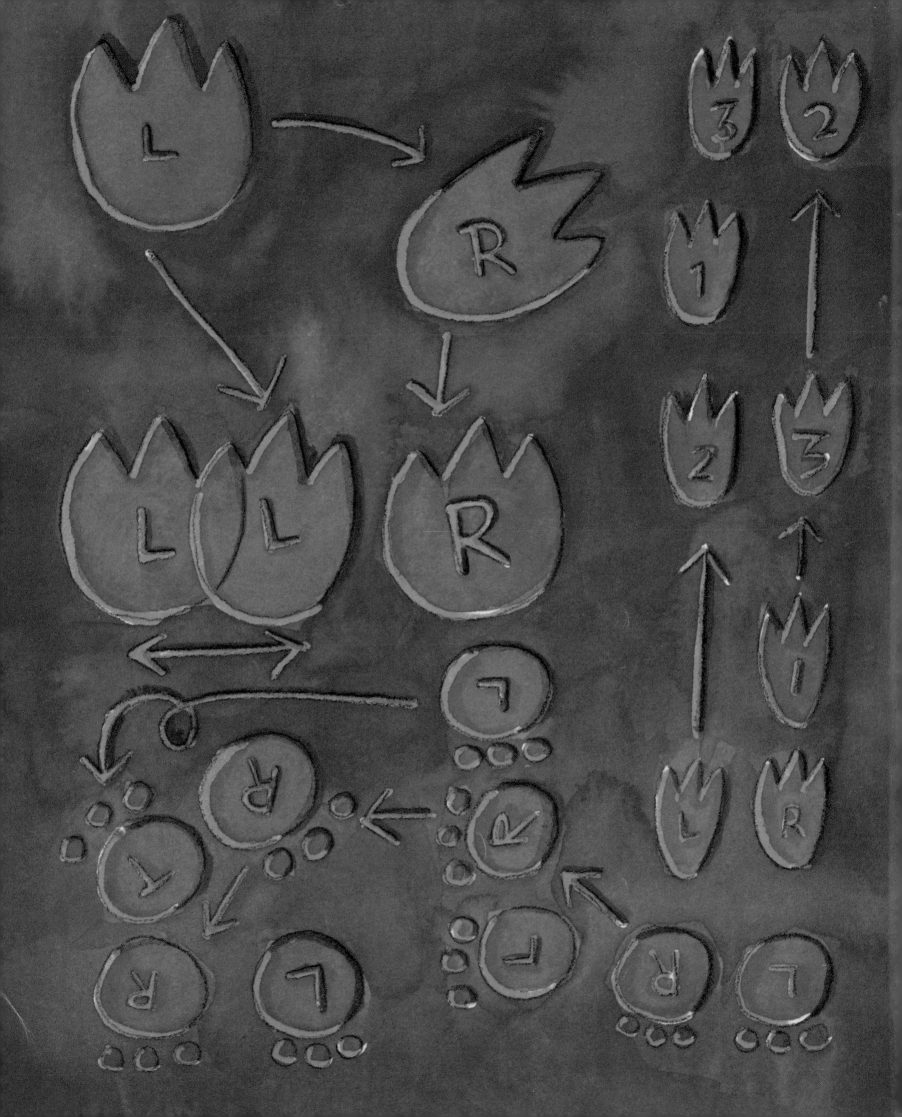

For Alex and Sam, with love
C. D. S.

To Sarah, Timmy, Allison, Charlie, and Nancy
S. N.

Text copyright © 1997 by Carol Diggory Shields
Illustrations copyright © 1997 by Scott Nash

All rights reserved. No part of this book may be reproduced, transmitted, or stored in an information retrieval
system in any form or by any means, graphic, electronic, or mechanical, including photocopying, taping, and
recording, without prior written permission from the publisher.

First U.S. paperback edition in this format 2008

The Library of Congress has cataloged the hardcover edition as follows:

Shields, Carol Diggory.
Saturday night at the dinosaur stomp / Carol Diggory Shields ; illustrated by Scott Nash. – 1st ed.
Summary: When it's rock 'n' roll time during the prehistoric era, many different kinds of dinosaurs
gather to twist, twirl, and tromp at a Saturday night party.
ISBN 978-1-56402-693-4 (hardcover)
[1. Dinosaurs – Fiction. 2. Parties – Fiction. 3. Stories in rhyme.]
I. Nash, Scott, date, ill. II. Title.
PZ8.3.S55365Sat 1997
[E]–dc21   97-536

ISBN 978-0-7636-0696-1 (paperback)
ISBN 978-0-7636-3887-0 (reformatted paperback)

09 10 11 12 13 14 SCP 10 9 8 7 6 5 4 3 2

Printed in Humen, Dongguan, China

This book was typeset in Cafeteria Bold.
The illustrations were done in watercolor and pencil.

Candlewick Press
99 Dover Street
Somerville, Massachusetts 02144

visit us at www.candlewick.com

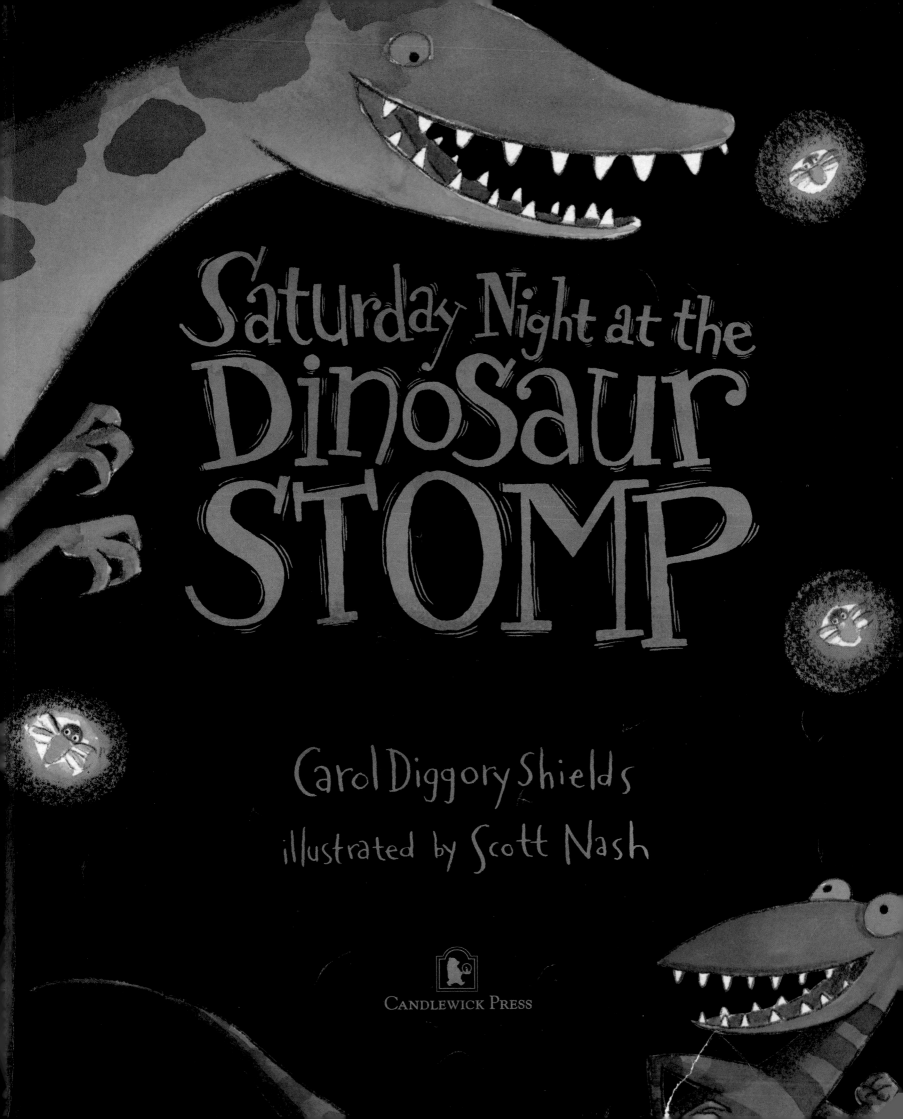

Saturday Night at the Dinosaur STOMP

Carol Diggory Shields

illustrated by Scott Nash

CANDLEWICK PRESS

Word went out 'cross the prehistoric slime:
"Hey, dinosaurs, it's rock 'n' roll time!
Slick back your scales and get ready to romp

By the lava beds and the tar pit shore,
On the mountaintop and the rain forest floor,

Dinosaurs scrubbed their necks and nails.
They brushed their teeth and curled their tails.

Then – ready, set, go – they trampled and tromped,

Making dinosaur tracks for the Dinosaur Stomp.

Plesiosaurus paddled up with a splash,

Protoceratops brought along her eggs,

A batch of bouncing babies followed Mama Maiasaur.

A pterodactyl family flew in for the bash.

Diplodocus plodded on big fat legs.

The last time she counted, she had twenty-four.

The old ones gathered in a gossiping bunch,
Sitting and sipping sweet Swampwater Punch.

Dinosaurs giggled and shuffled and stared,
Ready to party, but a little bit scared.

Then Iguanodon shouted, "One, *two*, three!"
Started up the band by waving a tree.

BOOMALACKA
BOOMALACKA!
WHACK!
WHACK!
WHACK!

Brachio-, Super-, and Ultrasaurus
Sang, "Doo-bop-a-loo-bop," in a chorus.
Ankylosaurus drummed on his hard-shelled back,
Boomalacka boomalacka! Whack! Whack!
Whack!

Pentaceratops stood up to perform
And blasted a tune on his favorite horn.

They played in rhythm, they sang in rhyme,
Dinosaur music in dinosaur time!

Duckbill thought he'd take a chance:
Asked Allosaurus if she'd like to dance.

Tarchia winked at a stegosaur she liked.
They danced together, spike to spike.

The Triassic Twist and the Brontosaurus Bump,
The Raptor Rap and Jurassic Jump.

Tyrannosaurus Rex led a conga line.

Carnosaurs capered close behind.

They rocked and rolled, they twirled and tromped.

There never was a party like the **Dinosaur Stomp.**

The nighttime sky began to glow.
Volcanoes put on a fireworks show.
The ground was rocking – it started to shake.
Those dinosaurs danced up the first earthquake!

The party went on – it was so outrageous,

They stayed up well past the late Cretaceous.

When the Cenozoic dawned they were tired and beat.
They yawned big yawns and put up their feet.

And they're *still* asleep, snoring deep in the swamp.
But they'll be back . . . next **Dinosaur Stomp!**

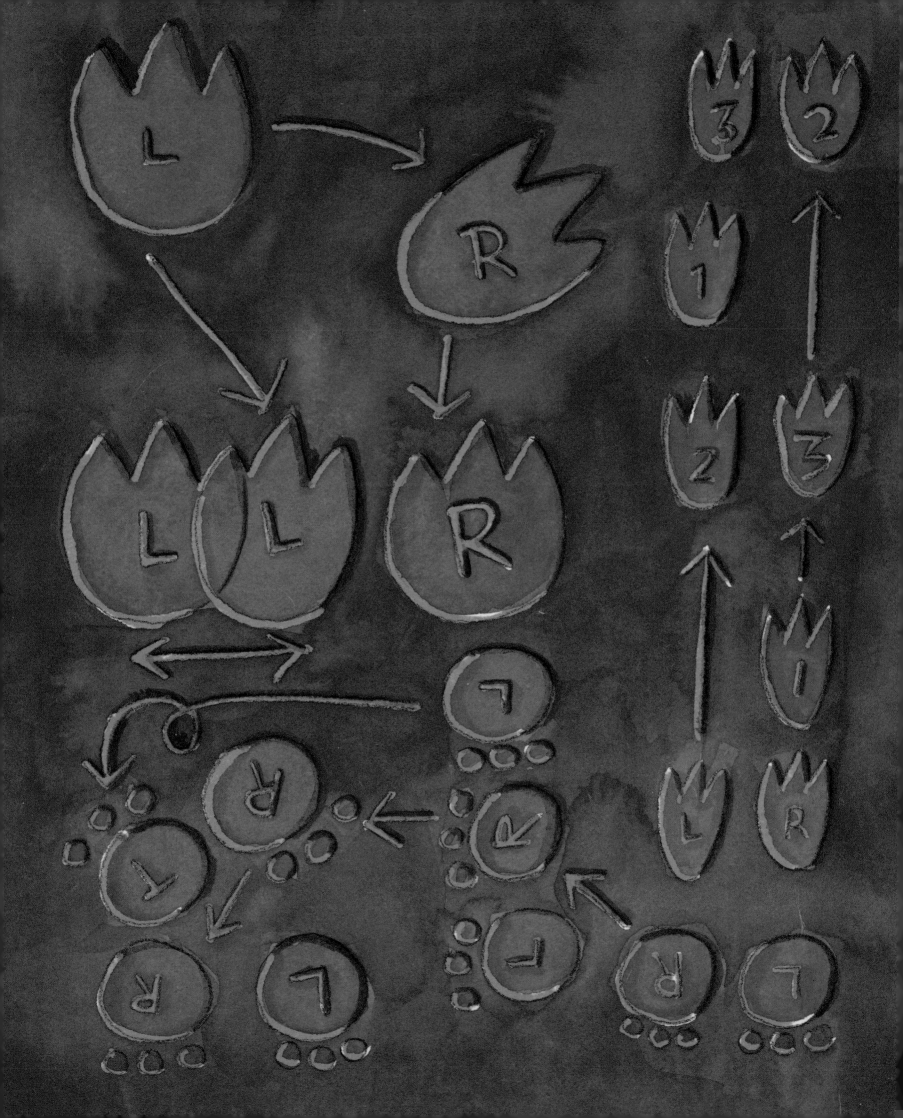

Carol Diggory Shields explains that she was inspired to write *Saturday Night at the Dinosaur Stomp* by "being called a Nagosaurus by my five-year-old. I started playing with the idea of partying dinosaurs who were scientifically accurate (more or less), and somehow in the prehistoric ooze of my brain, *Saturday Night at the Dinosaur Stomp* took shape." She also wrote *The Bugliest Bug*, illustrated by Scott Nash. Carol Diggory Shields lives in California.

Scott Nash once thought, "Poor dinosaurs. They always look so stiff and bored in books." In *Saturday Night at the Dinosaur Stomp*, he wanted to let them have some fun—his illustrations leap off the page like a raptor doing the fandango! However, when drawing for children, Scott is quick to admit if he does not know how to draw the dinosaur requested of him. "When you are talking with kids, you are dealing with dinosaur experts," he says. Scott Nash is also the illustrator of *The Bugliest Bug* by Carol Diggory Shields and the Brand New Readers *Monkey Business* and *Monkey Trouble* by David Martin, and he is the author-illustrator of *Tuff Fluff: The Case of Duckie's Missing Brain*. Scott Nash is the cofounder of Big Blue Dot, a design studio specializing in children's products and media. He lives in Maine.